One Fox

A COUNTING BOOK THRILLER

Kate Read

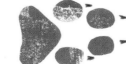

TWO HOOTS

1

One
famished
fox

2

Two sly eyes

3

Three
plump
hens

4

four
padding
paws

5

Five
snug
eggs

6 Six silent steps

Eight
beady
eyes

9 Nine
flying
feathers

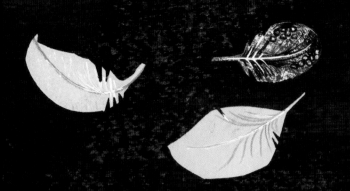

10

Ten
sharp teeth

100 One hundred angry hens and . . .

. . . one frightened fox.

No hens or foxes were harmed
in the making of this book.